Dear mouse friends,
Welcome to the world of

Geronimo Stilton

THE RODENT'S GAZETTE
EDITORIAL STAFF

Geronimo Stilton
A learned and brainy
mouse; editor of
The Rodent's Gazette

Thea Stilton
Geronimo's sister and
special correspondent at
The Rodent's Gazette

Trap Stilton
An awful joker;
Geronimo's cousin and
owner of the store
Cheap Junk for Less

Benjamin Stilton
A sweet and loving
nine-year-old mouse;
Geronimo's favorite
nephew

Geronimo Stilton

WEDDING CRASHER

Scholastic Inc.

New York   Toronto   London   Auckland   Sydney
Mexico City   New Delhi   Hong Kong   Buenos Aires

No part of this publication may be reproduced, or transmitted in any form or by any means, electronic, mechanical, photocopying, recording, or otherwise, without written permission of the publisher. For information regarding permission, write to Scholastic Inc., Attention: Permissions Department, 557 Broadway, New York, NY 10012.

ISBN 13: 978-0-439-84119-1
ISBN 10: 0-439-84119-4

Published by Scholastic Inc.
SCHOLASTIC and associated logos are trademarks and/or registered trademarks of Scholastic Inc.

Stilton is the name of a famous English cheese. It is a registered trademark of the Stilton Cheese Makers' Association. For more information, go to www.stiltoncheese.com.

Text by Geronimo Stilton
Original title: *Benvenuti a Rocca Taccagna*
Cover by Lorenzo Chiavini
Illustrations by Roberto Ronchi, Christian Aliprandi and Davide Turotti
Graphics by Merenguita Gingermouse and Michela Battaglin

Special thanks to Kathryn Cristaldi

12 11 10 9 8 7 6 5 4 3 2 1   7 8 9 10 11 12/0

Printed in the U.S.A.
First printing, January 2007

GERONIMO STILTON, RATTUS EMERITUS

That morning, everything started ringing at once. The toaster oven, the phone, the doorbell. I let the answering machine pick up the call, grabbed my cheesy toast from the toaster, and ran for the door. An Express Mail mouse stood on my doorstep.

"Letter for you, Mr. Stilton,"
he squeaked, pawing me a strange-looking
envelope. "The sender has requested you
pay for the postage."

I grumbled, pulling out my wallet. **How rude!** What kind of mouse can't pay for stamps?

After the mail mouse left, I looked more closely at the envelope. It was made out of old scraps of newspaper glued together. **How Strange!**

Geronimo Stilton, Rattus Emeritus, it read. I started to open the envelope. That's when I realized it was sealed with *A PIECE OF STICKY CHEWING GUM.* Slimy Swiss balls! **How disgusting!**

Inside, I found a greasy note. I sniffed it. It smelled like an old cheese wrapper. And not in a good way.

The note was written in **crayon**. It looked like it had been written by a mouselet! It appeared to be a wedding invitation, but it didn't look like any wedding invitation I'd ever seen before. I squinted at it, and couldn't believe my eyes! It said:

Geronimo Stilton,
Rattus Emeritus
8 Mouseford Lane
New Mouse City,
Mouse Island

Samuel S. Stingysnout
Is pleased to invite

Geronimo Stilton

to the wedding of his son,

Stevie Stingysnout,
to
Patience Plainpaws.

The ceremony will be held
at the family home,
Penny Pincher Castle
on Cheap Change Hill.

Gift Required.

ARE YOU PACKED?

Ah, yes, Uncle Samuel S. Stingysnout. Who else would send a wedding invitation written on an old cheese wrapper and sealed with chewing gum? Uncle Samuel S. Stingysnout was the cheapest mouse I had ever met. When he had a cold, he refused to buy tissues. Instead, he blew his nose into his tail. Yuck!

I called my sister, Thea, to see if she had gotten an invitation, too.

Oh, I got one.

"Oh, I GOT ONE," Thea snorted. "I put a clothespin

on my nose before I opened it. Cheese niblets, what a stench! So are you packed?"

I couldn't believe it. Thea actually wanted to go to the **STINGYSNOUT** wedding?

"Of course we're going," my sister insisted. "Uncle Samuel may be cheap, but he lives in a castle. We've never been there before. It will be fun! I'll be over with Benjamin and Trap in a few minutes to get you."

"Now?!" I shrieked. But there was no answer. As usual, Thea had hung up on me.

I bit my tail to keep from

SCREAMING!!!

Why, oh, why did my sister try to drive me crazy? She knew I was a planner. I liked to

prepare before I went off on a trip. I liked to pack carefully. What if I forgot my tie? What if I forgot my toothbrush? What if a late winter storm hit and I needed my catfur earmuffs?

Ten minutes later, Thea was at my place. "Ready?" she squeaked.

I opened my mouth to say no. But just then, my favorite nephew, Benjamin, grabbed my paw.

Do you like it?

"Oh, this is so exciting, Uncle Geronimo! I've never been to a wedding before. Look at the wedding present I made. Do you like it?" he cried.

He showed me two small red cardboard hearts with the names of the bride and groom on them. I sighed. How could I say no to my dear, sweet nephew?

I threw some stuff in my suitcase and followed my family out the door.

with the names of the bride and groom on them. He showed me two small red cardboard hearts

WHAT A PLACE!

It was a long trip.

A VERY, VERY LONG ONE.

Uncle Samuel S. Stingysnout's castle was far outside of New Mouse City. We passed through wooded forests, rocky mountains, and fields filled with nothing but high brown grass. There was not a store or newspaper stand in sight. What a nightmare! I guess you could say Uncle Samuel lived in the middle of nowhere.

Finally, we spotted the castle. It was perched on the top of a large hill. The castle seemed to be built out of all different materials — brick, stone, glass, Silly Putty. It looked like a RODENT put it together with his eyes closed. Old

The castle seemed to be built out of all different materials.

aluminium cans were crushed into one side of the building, and the windows were all different shapes and sizes.

A flag hung over the castle entrance. It showed a faded and patched coat of arms that read, PENNY PINCHER CASTLE.

The flag also had a picture of a mouse holding a piggy bank in his paw.

As we drew closer, we realized there was a moat surrounding the castle. The water smelled like my grandma Onewhisker's DISGUSTING Swiss cheese casserole. It was as thick as pea soup, only instead of being pea green, this water was brown.

I clutched my stomach. Did I mention that I have a weak digestive system?

"How are we supposed to get through *that*?" Trap squeaked, holding his nose.

THERE WAS A MOAT SURROUNDING THE CASTLE THAT SMELLED DISGUSTING.

Thea smirked. "Must we females do everything?" she huffed. Then she put her paw in her mouth and let out an ear-piercing whistle. I thought my head would explode! CHEESE NIBLETS! Did I mention that I have sensitive ears?

Instantly, a small door opened up right above the water level. A thin mouse's snout peeked out.

"Well, well, well, here they are at last, my dear, dear relatives . . . **Welcome to the most beautiful place on Earth, Penny Pincher Castle!**"

called my uncle Samuel S. Stingysnout.

I nibbled my whiskers to keep from squeaking. The most beautiful place on Earth? I wondered if my uncle had ever seen an **EYE** doctor. Maybe I should tell him about my optometrist, Dr. Bifocals.

But before I had a chance, Uncle Samuel began paddling toward us in an old, patched up inner tube.

"Climb aboard my private ferry," he instructed.

I stared at the leaking tube. It was deflating by the second. Private ferry? Was he kidding?

Uncle Samuel waved a paw at the smelly water. "Ah, yes, isn't this place fabulous?" he boasted. "All the comforts of a luxury resort.

FEEL FREE TO SWIM IN THE SPARKLING WATERS, IF YOU WISH."

I tried not to laugh out loud.

We paddled past clumps of foul-smelling water plants, old cheese rinds, and plastic milk bottles. WHAT A DUMP! The only thing sparkling in these waters were the aluminium cans and other bits of junk.

My eyes began to tear. Did I mention that I'm allergic to foul-smelling garbage?

IT ITCHES, IT ITCHES, IT ITCHES!

I clutched the sides of the tube and tried not to think about my watering eyes or sour stomach. Every now and then, a splash of **smelly** moat water hit me in the face. Moldy mozzarella!

WHY, OH WHY had I agreed to come on this trip? I was a good mouse. I never hurt anyone. Well, there was that one time I clocked my uncle Handypaws in the snout with a golf club. But it was an accident. I didn't hear him scamper up behind me.

I was still thinking about Uncle Handypaws when my tail began to itch. I tried scratching, but the itching only got worse. Suddenly, I was scratching away like a mad mouse.

"It itches! It itches! It itcheeesss!"
I shrieked.

Finally, I couldn't take it anymore. I tore off my pants to make the scratching easier.

That's when I noticed that a crowd of rodents had gathered outside the castle. "Look at that mouse! What's he doing in his underwear?" I heard one say.

"*HOW SHAMEFUL!*" another added.

"**How tacky!**" squeaked a third.

When we reached the other side of the moat, Thea gave me an annoyed look.

"Why do you have to be so embarrassing, Geronimo?" she whispered.

Just then, I heard Trap snicker under his whiskers, "IT WORKS! THE ITCHING POWDER REALLY WORKS!"

Itching powder? I should have known. My obnoxious cousin loves to play pranks — especially on yours truly! I was livid. If only I could get my paws on him. But he disappeared into the castle before I had a chance.

I climbed out of the tube and entered the courtyard, which was CROWDED with guests.

They were all staring at me.

I could hear them murmuring. "Is it possible? Can that shameful mouse really be Geronimo Stilton? The famouse publisher?" I heard one mouse say.

"It is!" another confirmed.

"How embarrassing, to have such a

relative!!!" a third squeaked.

By now, I was red with anger.

I marched up to Trap in the main hall of the castle. I was going to give him a piece of my mind.

But as soon as I opened my mouth, Trap shoved something into it. Something sweet. Something gooey. Something chocolate!

I love **chocolate**!

Is it possible? The famouse publisher! How embarrassing!

"Sorry about the itching incident," Trap squeaked. "Hope you like the chocolate."

I was in shock. It's not like my cousin to apologize.

But I didn't have much time to think about it, because Uncle Samuel S. Stingysnout's excited squeak broke into my thoughts. "Welcome, dear guests!" he exclaimed.

What's he doing?

Can that mouse really be Geronimo Stilton?

"Welcome to my
magnificent home!"

A NICE WARM ROOM

We followed Uncle Samuel up a LONG, winding, crumbling, staircase. He stopped at a door covered with worm holes.

"This, dear nephews, is your room," he squeaked proudly, flinging open the door for me, Trap, and Benjamin. "You can freshen up while I show Thea to her room. We'll meet in a half hour in the banquet hall."

I blinked. The room was a sight for poor eyes. AND I MEAN REALLY POOR!

The paint was chipping off the walls. The floor was covered with a patched-up cheddar yellow carpet. And the rotted bookcase looked like it was about to collapse.

Benjamin took down one of the books.

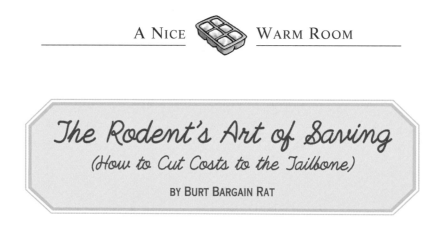

The Rodent's Art of Saving
(How to Cut Costs to the Tailbone)

BY BURT BARGAIN RAT

He tried to open it but couldn't. The book wasn't real. It was just a block of wood!

I couldn't believe it. I was still staring at the block of wood when Trap began to shriek.

"**Yowee!**" he cried. He had tried to sit down on a faded leather pawchair, and a spring had poked him right in the tail.

I headed for the window. Maybe a little light would help cheer up this gloomy place. But when I tried to open the curtains, I couldn't. They were painted right onto the wall!

Just then, I caught sight of some flames burning in the fireplace. How strange. The room felt like the **freezer** in the back room of the Icy Rat ice cream parlor!

I stretched my paws toward the **flames**. That's when I realized they weren't flames at all. They were just strips of red paper being blown around by the ice-cold air.

I shivered. Did I mention that I'm not a cold weather mouse?

Oh, why had I come to this awful, freezing place?!

The room felt like the freezer of
the ice cream parlor.

WHERE'S THE BATHROOM?

I flipped open my suitcase and immediately began to unpack. My sister calls me a **neatnick**. That's because I like to have everything in its place all the time — underwear, socks, my Cheeseball the Clown night-light. I had just finished hanging up my jacket when I heard a strange rumbling noise. It was my tummy.

All of a sudden, I felt like my stomach was about to explode.

"Where's the bathroom?" I shrieked. "**I have to go!**" I lurched out into the hall and grabbed the bathroom doorknob. Rat-munching rattlesnakes! It wouldn't open!

"Look, Uncle Geronimo, there's a sign on the door," Benjamin said. Then he read the tiny letters out loud.

"If you need to use the bathroom, please ask for the key. Sincerely, *Samuel S. Stingysnout.*"

"But I can't wait!" I cried, clutching my gurgling stomach. "Help!"

Benjamin took off down the stairs. "Don't worry, Uncle! I'll get the key and be right back!" he shouted.

I stumbled back into the room in a daze. That's when I noticed Trap rolling on the floor, laughing. He was holding a box in his paws. Something told me that it wasn't a get-well present for me. I stared at the label on the box. It said, **TRICK CHOCOLATES.**

"What a great prank! That little piece of chocolate worked IN RECORD TIME!" my cousin chuckled.

I was furious. "You're going to pay for this!" I squeaked. But first, I had to find the key to the bathroom. I staggered out the door. Where, oh where was Uncle Samuel?

THE KEY! THE KEY!

I raced down the hall, turned a corner, and ran smack into my uncle.

"The key! The key, please!" I shouted, panting. My stomach was gurgling so loudly that I could barely hear myself squeak.

Unfortunately, my uncle couldn't hear me, either. He could hear about as well as a block of stale cheese. "Eh? What? *Some tea?*" he asked, cupping his ear.

"The **key**! The **bathroom** key!" I tried again.

He stared at me, confused. "The tree? You've seen a bonsai tree?" he guessed.

I wanted to cry. I wanted to scream. I wanted to grab my uncle by the tail and fling him up to the moon.

Luckily, just then Benjamin arrived. "He needs the key to the bathroom," he explained loudly.

My uncle sniffed. "Well, why didn't he say so?" he squeaked. "Now, let's see. Where did I put that key? In the kitchen, or maybe in the study, or maybe . . ."

I couldn't take it anymore. "**JUST FIND IT!**" I shrieked at the top of my lungs.

At that moment, I noticed all of the doors to the other guests' rooms were open. Everyone was staring at me in horror from their doorways.

"Who is making all that fuss?" I heard one rodent ask.

"It's that Geronimo Stilton again," another answered.

"What a perfectly **DREADFUL** mouse!" a third cried.

"**Inexcusable!**" a fourth added.

Right then, Uncle Samuel remembered that the bathroom key was hanging from a nail in the greenhouse, so we headed down to the garden.

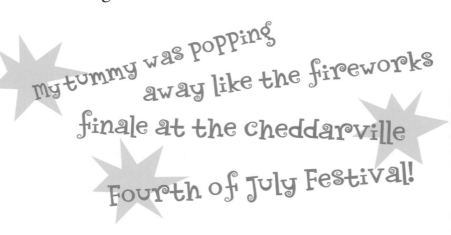

My tummy was popping away like the fireworks finale at the cheddarville Fourth of July Festival!

I did an impatient little dance behind a rose bush in the garden, WAITING, WAITING, WAITING. I couldn't wait much longer! What seemed like hours later, Uncle Samuel strolled out of the greenhouse waving a brass key. "See, I told you it was in

Waiting, waiting, waiting...

the greenhouse," he announced triumphantly. He gave Benjamin the key.

As I raced back up the castle steps, I was fuming. I couldn't stop thinking about Trap and those **trick chocolates**. What a dirty rotten trick! How dare he make a fool out of me! I hurled myself up the last few stairs. I couldn't wait to get my paws on my prankster cousin.

But I *really* couldn't wait to get to the bathroom.

I hurled myself up the last few stairs.

PATIENCE PLAINPAWS

After I finally got in and out of the bathroom, I stormed into the living room. It was crowded with chattering guests. I recognized a few distant relatives, but I had no time for small squeak. I only had one rodent on my mind. Just then, I spotted my cousin at the far side of the room. I pushed through the crowd like a madmouse.

"**What's all this pushing?**" a gray rodent grumbled.

"It's that Geronimo Stilton again!" a mouse in a feathered hat announced.

"*He stomped right on my tail!*" squeaked a short rat.

I felt bad. I really am a true gentlemouse. But I was so enraged

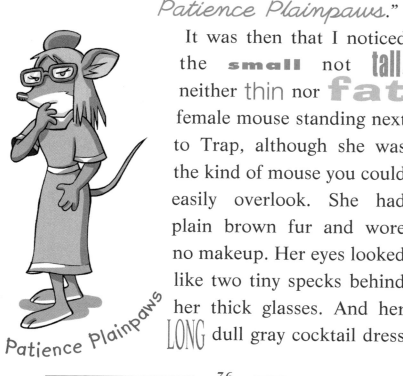

that I could barely see straight. Just as I reached Trap, he whirled around. He had a huge smile on his snout.

"There you are, **Gerry Berry**, my favorite cousin," Trap gushed. "I'd like you to meet the charming young bride-to-be, *Patience Plainpaws*."

It was then that I noticed the **small** not **tall**, neither thin nor **fat** female mouse standing next to Trap, although she was the kind of mouse you could easily overlook. She had plain brown fur and wore no makeup. Her eyes looked like two tiny specks behind her thick glasses. And her LONG dull gray cocktail dress

Patience Plainpaws

hung on her like a sack.

She wasn't ugly, but she wasn't beautiful. She was just . . . **plain**.

"Ahem . . . I am . . . I mean, my name is . . . um, that is . . . I am Patience Plainpaws," she whispered awkwardly.

I shook her paw. "Pleased to meet you," I started to say, but I was interrupted by a tall, thin rat. He wore glasses, too, and a bowtie around his neck. His yellowish fur was thinning on top, even though he wasn't that old. In fact, he'd probably be calling the Fur Club for Mice in a few years. Yep, my cousin Stevie Stingysnout was definitely on the road to baldness.

"Dear cousin Geronimo, how are you?" he asked warmly, slapping me on the back. "I'm so pleased. No, I'm honored. No, I'm **OVERJOYED** to see you!"

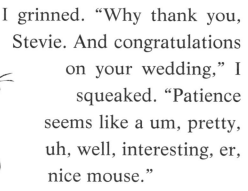

At last, someone who appreciated me. Someone who knew I was an **important** mouse. I am the publisher of the most popular newspaper in New Mouse City, after all.

I grinned. "Why thank you, Stevie. And congratulations on your wedding," I squeaked. "Patience seems like a um, pretty, uh, well, interesting, er, nice mouse."

Stevie curled his whiskers.

For some reason, he had a strangely smug expression on his snout. "Yes, poor plain Patience," he murmured. "She is

Stevie Stingysnout

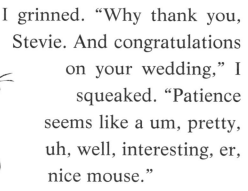

rather dull, but she adores me, of course. Who wouldn't?"

I chewed my *whisker* to keep from snorting. Who did Stevie think he was? The famouse movie star, **Brad Ratt**? I had never met such a pompous rodent before!

Then Stevie leaned closer. "I was wondering if you could take a look at an amazing book I have written. It's called *Memoirs of a Perfect Rodent* and it's all about me. I want you to publish it."

I sighed. Now I knew why my cousin was being so nice to me. He wanted me to print his ridiculous book!

HOPE YOU LIKE BATHROOMS!

Stevie **SQUEAKED** on and on about his book. His voice reminded me of my uncle Cheesebelly's automatic cheese slicer. It droned on forever! I thought I would faint from boredom. Then I spotted my cousin Trap chatting with Patience Plainpaws. But wait! He wasn't just talking. He was holding what looked like a box of chocolates. **I gulped.** Had my cousin gone mad? Why would he give the bride-to-be a **trick chocolate**? She'd be stuck in the bathroom on one of the most important days of her life!

I watched in **horror** as Patience brought the candy to her mouth.

It was so sad. It was so pathetic. It was so wrong.

Right then, I decided I had to do something. I had to save Patience.

With a squeak, I scampered across the room and snatched the chocolate from the little mouse's paws. I shoved it into Trap's mouth instead.

"**There you go!**" I shouted. "Let's see how *you* like eating your trick chocolates, Trap. **Hope you like bathrooms!**"

I JUMPED ON THE BOX, CRUSHING IT TO PIECES.

The chocolates that missed Trap's mouth scattered across the floor.

Just thinking about those **CHoCoLaTeS** made me mad enough to twist my tail up in knots. I threw the box on the floor. Then I **JUMpED** on it, crushing it to pieces.

A hush fell over the room.

I looked up. Everyone was staring at me. As for my cousin, he calmly chewed the chocolate and swallowed.

Then he popped three more into his mouth.

"Delicious!" he exclaimed. By now, his snout was covered in chocolate. "I don't know why you didn't want me to give Stevie and Patience these chocolates," he smirked.

"I bought this box at Select Sweets, the finest candy store in all of New Mouse City."

Then he lowered his voice and winked.

"Of course, what you had was a different kind of chocolate altogether, Gerry Berry," he chuckled.

I stared at my paws and felt my cheeks grow red. I felt lower than a sewer rat.

The crowd around me began to murmur.

"That Geronimo Stilton is starting to get under my fur," one mouse squeaked.

"Did you see the wild look in his eyes when he crushed the chocolate box?" another commented.

"I think the cheese has really slid off his cracker," a third said.

I was so humiliated, **red with shame.** All of these rodents thought I was nuts. Could things get any worse?

DON'T SPOIL
YOUR APPETITE!

A few minutes later, Uncle Samuel S. Stingysnout called everyone into the dining room. He held up his paw for silence. Then he made a speech. "Dear *beloved* relatives, the wedding ceremony will take place just three days from now. Tonight we will have what I like to call a light dinner. This way you will not spoil your appetite for the grand wedding *celebration*!"

We scrambled to take our seats at the very long table.

We were all starving. We hadn't eaten a regular meal since we left home.

"It's about time we nibbled some cheese!" Trap grumbled, *knotting* his napkin around his neck.

It's about time we nibbled some cheese!

My cousin Stevie was **grumbling**, too. Only he wasn't grumbling about food. He was grumbling about his future bride.

"Well, don't just stand there, Patience," he complained. "Go and get us some drinks. And don't forget to put on an apron so you don't get that new dress **dirty**."

I couldn't believe it. My cousin was ordering the poor mouse around like she was a lowly sewer rat.

"If he were my fiancé, I'd dump him like a stick of **MOLDY** cheese," Thea murmured.

"He's so mean, and she's so *kind*," Benjamin added, looking confused.

A few minutes later, Patience returned from the kitchen. She was wearing a WHITE apron and maid's cap. She made her way around the table passing out the appetizer, a glass of tap water.

None of the guests seemed to notice Patience Plainpaws. They were too busy gossiping. I guess you could say I was eavesdropping, but I couldn't help it. EVERYONE WAS SQUEAKING about the same thing, the bride and her lost fortune. Yes, it seemed that Patience Plainpaws used to be rolling in the dough. And I'm not talking about the kind of dough you find at The Slice Rat pizzeria.

Patience grew up in a poor family. They lived in a small mouse hole on the rundown side of town. Her father was an inventor, but none of his inventions ever seemed to work out. Then one day, he created a unique cheese-scented perfume. He called it Scent of Swiss. It became a huge hit! Before long, the Plainpaws family had made a fortune. They moved into a bigger mouse hole and began traveling all over the world.

Then **TRAGEDY** struck. Mr. and Mrs. Plainpaws disappeared while hot-air ballooning over the Mousehara Desert. Patience became an orphan, and she was poor once again. That's because Mr. and Mrs. Plainpaws didn't believe in banks. They had hidden their **FORTUNE** somewhere near their mouse hole. Unfortunately, Patience was still looking for it to this day.

"How sad. She's such a plain, UNATTRACTIVE MOUSE," I heard one guest comment.

"It's not surprising she's marrying Stevie.

Who else would want such a **dreary mouse**?" another added.

I watched Patience shyly passing out the glasses of water. Just then, she accidentally knocked one over.

"Now look what you've done, you clumsy mouse!" Stevie scolded her. "You really must learn to be more careful."

Patience nodded, looking embarrassed.

Next to me, my sister stamped her foot. **"How dare he speak to her that way!"**

she fumed. She looked like she was about to
EXPLODE.

Oh, no, I thought. Once my sister gets all riled up, there's no stopping her. One time, her friend Swissita had her purse stolen. Thea ran after the thief and snatched back the purse. Then she tied the robber's tail to a lamppost on the corner of Cat Cross Boulevard.

Lucky for Stevie, Uncle Samuel S. Stingysnout's castle was miles away from the boulevard.

WHAT'S WITH THE CHAINS?

I kept an eye on Thea as I sipped my water. There was barely enough water in the glass to wet my whiskers. I stared at my plate. It was rusty and dented. A TINY square of white cloth lay under my fork. I guess my uncle was too cheap to spring for a whole napkin.

When I tried to lift my fork, it wouldn't budge. That's when I realized that each piece of silverware was attached to a small chain. The chains were nailed to the floor.

"What's with the chains?" Trap griped.

Thea rolled her EYES. "I think Old Stingysnout is afraid we're going to steal his silverware," she said.

I picked up my fork. It clanked against the chain. I felt like I was having dinner in the mess hall at Tough Squeak Prison. Have you ever been there? It's one scary place. The rodents at Tough Squeak are so mean that even their own mothers are AFRAID of them.

I was thinking about the prison when Patience suddenly appeared at the head of the table. She was carrying a large SILVER

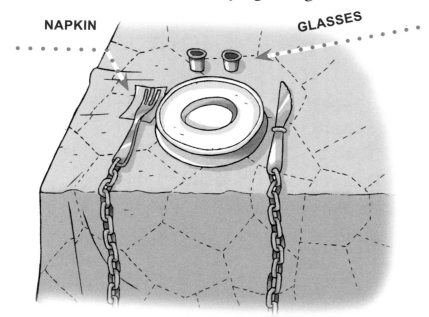

NAPKIN

GLASSES

serving tray. The tray had a big silver cover over it. **Food!**

The room fell silent. Well, except for Trap's rumbling tummy. Everyone stared at the silver platter hungrily.

"Hooray, we eat at last!" squeaked Benjamin.

BRUSSELS SPROUTS AND BANANA PEELS

Uncle Samuel held up his paw again for silence. "And now, the moment you have all been waiting for!" he announced in a loud voice. He motioned for Patience to begin passing out the food.

By now, my stomach was rumbling just like my cousin's. How embarrassing! I sounded like a race car at full speed. Visions of cheddar melts and gooey Cheesy Chews danced through my head.

I was so busy dreaming about food, I didn't even notice that Patience had rounded the table. A second later, she dropped a tiny speck of something onto my plate. What was it? Did she lose a button? I squinted to

get a better look.

"We will begin with **one** stuffed pea," Old Stingysnout **squeaked**.

One stuffed pea? I stared at my plate in disbelief.

How do you stuff a pea? I was too hungry to ask. Instead, I stabbed at the pea with my fork. But it was so tiny that I missed. It shot off my plate and onto the floor.

"Finders keepers!" Trap shouted, scooping up my pea. He popped it into his mouth.

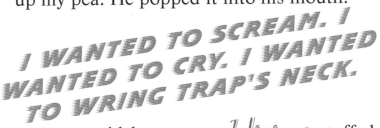

I WANTED TO SCREAM. I WANTED TO CRY. I WANTED TO WRING TRAP'S NECK.

How could he eat my *delicious* stuffed pea? Okay, it was only a pea, but I was desperate. Desperate for food. What was next? A rotten banana peel for the main course?

To my relief, Patience disappeared into the kitchen and came out with a second covered silver platter. My spirits soared. Forget the pea, maybe there were grilled **cheese** sandwiches under there. Or **blue cheese** danishes. Or MOZZARELLA milk shakes.

"Our second course will feature **one** delicious boiled brussels sprout. And for dessert, everyone will receive **one** yummy raspberry," Uncle Samuel squeaked proudly.

Tears sprang to my eyes. I took my glasses off so I could cry freely.

A MISHMASH OF USELESS JUNK

After dinner, the guests watched as the bride and groom opened their gifts. There were **crystal** goblets, **UGLY** lamps, and a pair of **cracked** candlesticks.

Patience cried when she unwrapped Benjamin's homemade cardboard hearts.

I felt like crying myself. Oh, why hadn't I insisted that Benjamin bring a nice fruit basket? Or a gourmet cheesecake? Or a block of day-old cheddar? Any sort of food!

Thea's **gift** was next. It was a leopard-spotted nightgown. The bride looked thrilled, but the groom frowned.

"Dear cousin," he coughed, "I'm afraid this is really not right for Patience. She's rather plain, if you know what I mean. I think she'd be better off in a nice woolen pair of long underwear. After all, the castle tends to be very **chilly** at night. We don't like to turn on the heat when it's cold. It costs money."

I shivered. Well, that explains why I felt like a walking **mousesicle**. I tried thinking warm thoughts. Sunny beaches, crackling fires . . . I closed my eyes. How strange. I could almost hear the fire crackling.

Then I realized it was just Trap. He had a habit of cracking his knuckles. **How rude!** Sometimes I can hardly believe we're related.

I was still thinking about my obnoxious cousin when Patience unwrapped my gift. It was a **SOLID GOLD** one-of-a-kind cheese dish.

"THANK YOU, THANK YOU, COUSIN!"

Stevie squeaked, grabbing the gift from Patience. "This thing must be worth a lot of money!"

I could tell Stevie couldn't wait to return my gift to the store in exchange for cash. Oh, well. Maybe with the money he would stop living in the arctic zone and turn on the heat in the castle once in a while.

At last, all of the gifts had been opened. What a mishmash of **useless junk!** There was a music box containing a statue of a mouse, a snow globe, an ugly tie, a silver toilet seat cover with ornate designs engraved on the top, and what looked like a **rotten** apple.

The gifts took up one whole corner of the room. It looked like a small flea market — minus the fleas. (Well, unless you counted the fruit flies *buzzing* around the apple thingy.)

THE FAMOUSE
UNCLE GAGRAT

After the presents, Uncle Stingysnout told everyone to relax in the living room. My stomach was still grumbling, but I decided to ignore it. So I hadn't eaten a thing all day. So I was feeling weak in the paws. I would live. After all, who ever heard of a rodent kicking the bucket after skipping a few meals? But just then, my tummy let out a loud **ROAR**. Headlines flashed through my brain: STILTON STARVES TO DEATH AT WEDDING! PUBLISHER PASSES OUT FROM HUNGER!

I rubbed my stomach to calm it down. That's when I noticed that the guests were all staring at me with **disgust**. I coughed.

I scampered to an old pawchair in the corner of the room.

But just as I sat down, I heard a loud, obnoxious sound.

Prrrrt! Prrrrt! Prrrrt! Prrrrt! Prrrrt!

My fur turned **BEET RED**. I jumped up.

The room fell silent.

Everyone was staring at me again. This time, they looked even more disgusted.

I'm going to get Trap for this, I thought. Who else would play such an embarrassing TRICK on me?

"That's it, Cousin!" I shrieked. "This time you've gone too far!"

I leaped across the room. But Trap was too fast. He climbed up onto the piano, out of reach. "It wasn't me, Germeister!" he protested.

Then I heard a *giggle* behind my back. I whirled around.

"How did you like my **joke**?" a rodent snickered.

I sighed. I should have known. It was my uncle Gagrat, the biggest prankster on two paws.

It wasn't me, Germeister!

CLOSE AND DISTANT RELATIVES

Uncle Gagrat pulled out a **RED BALLOON** from under my chair. He waved it in the air.

"Pretty good, eh, Nephew?" he chuckled. He slapped me on the back so hard I nearly lost my whiskers.

"Ahem, very funny, Uncle," I mumbled, still embarrassed.

The whole room was now laughing at me.

Oh, why did everyone like to pick on me? I was a good mouse. I didn't lie, cheat, or steal. Well, except for the time I took a box of **cheese crackers** from the grocery store. But it was an accident. Sometimes I forget to look in the bottom of my shopping cart. I was still thinking about those yummy crackers when I spotted Aunt Sugarfur.

Squeaking of yummy, my aunt Sugarfur always smelled like a yummy batch of homemade cookies. That's because she ran her own bakery for years and years.

"How are you, Auntie?" I squeaked, giving her a mouse-sized hug. Oh, how I love dear *Aunt Sugarfur*. Every time I visit her, she gives me a delicious triple chocolate cheese muffin.

Now she pulled one out of her purse. "This is for you, Geronimo," she said, grinning.

Aunt Sugarfur

I felt like I died and went to mouse heaven.

Food! I swallowed that muffin in one gulp.

Behind Aunt Sugarfur was her husband, Uncle Kindpaws, and their twins, Squeakette and Squeaky. My cousins were dressed in matching **yellow tutus.**

They danced over to Benjamin. "Go play with them," I encouraged him. My nephew can be a little shy at first.

Next I was greeted by my uncle Walter Worrywhiskers. Uncle Wally is a champion worrywart. Every month, he is convinced he has another rare and awful disease.

"How are you, Uncle Wally?" I asked, shaking his paw.

His fur paled. "Why do you ask?" he stammered. "Do I look ill? Are my whiskers drooping? Is my tail twitching?"

*Squeakette and Squeaky were dressed
in matching yellow tutus.*

Before I could answer, he whipped out an antibacterial wipe. He carefully cleaned his paws, face, tail, and **ears**.

Just then, another uncle tapped me on the back. It was Uncle Mastermouse. Uncle Mastermouse was a top professor at New Mouse City University. He could rattle on and on for hours about *anything*. The only problem was he liked to talk about the most boring subjects on earth, like cheese graters and pawnail clippers.

HE COULD PUT A MOUSE TO SLEEP WITH ONE SENTENCE.

THE EARLY MOUSE
CATCHES THE CHEESE

That night, I wished I had Uncle Mastermouse around to put me to sleep. I barely slept a wink. It was **fur-freezing cold.** I tried pretending the fake fireplace was real. But it didn't help. My teeth were still chattering.

I huddled under an old HOLEY blanket, fully dressed. I was even wearing my coat! On top of it all, the bed had no mattress. Uncle Samuel claimed that sleeping on a board is healthier for your back. "A mouse needs good posture," he explained. I tossed and turned all night.

Forget good posture! This mouse just needed a good night's sleep.

At *five* in the morning, Old Stingysnout woke everyone up. He was standing in the garden courtyard. "Time to wake up, dear relatives!" he screamed into a megaphone.

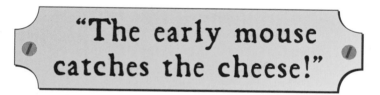

"The early mouse catches the cheese!"

In the bed next to me, Trap pulled the blanket up to his snout. "Cheese," he grumbled. **"I'll believe that when I see it.** If he serves brussels sprouts for breakfast, I'm out of here."

We trooped down to the kitchen.

Uncle Samuel was busy explaining to Patience how to recycle tea bags.

"It's all in the wrist, my dear. You must dip the tea bag into the hot water for the briefest of moments, and then pull it out. **Zap!** Like this!" he instructed, demonstrating. "You'll see, with this method, your tea bags will last you for ages."

Patience stared at the tea bag as if in a trance. I wondered what she was thinking.

Meanwhile, Uncle Samuel was keeping an eye on all the hungry relatives roaming the kitchen.

"Breakfast will be ready soon," he announced. "Everyone please have a seat."

My mouth began to water. I could go for a tasty egg-and-cheese sandwich on a sesame seed bun. Or maybe even a nice warm stack of cheddar pancakes. I picked up a jar of strawberry jam in the center of the table. Yum!

In a flash, Old Stingysnout appeared at my side. "PLEASE PUT THAT DOWN, GERONIMO," he ordered.

"IT'S FOR DECORATION ONLY."

Two minutes later, Uncle Samuel served us our breakfast. It didn't take long. We each got one tiny bread crumb.

"Nothing like a whole grain in the morning," my uncle said, sighing happily.

GREAT-GRANDFATHER CHEDDAR CHEAPSKATE

This time, my tummy wasn't the only one grumbling. Everyone had had it with Uncle Samuel S. Stingysnout's stingy ways. Of course, my uncle didn't even seem to notice.

"Ah, it's so nice to have all my dear relatives here," he said, beaming. "It reminds me of the **family reunion** we used to have when my great-grandfather was alive. Yes, Great-Grandfather Cheddar Cheapskate. Now *there* was a mouse who knew how to save his pennies and his bread crumbs. He taught me everything I know about economizing."

With a sigh, Uncle Samuel wiped away a small tear.

"Old Cheapskate could make a roll of toilet paper last six months. He could cut a cheese morsel one hundred ways," he boasted. "He was an artist, a true saver, a . . ."

Great-Grandfather Cheddar Cheapskate

Before he could go on, my cousin Squeakette whirled into the kitchen. "Uncle Samuel," she interrupted. "The hot water isn't working! How am I supposed to shampoo, rinse, and repeat, not to mention condition?"

Uncle Samuel smiled under his whiskers. "Ah, my dear, I'm so sorry! It was working up until the moment you arrived," he insisted.

Something told me he wasn't exactly telling the truth. In fact, he was probably lying through his teeth. After all, Old Stingysnout needed to turn on the electricity in order to make the water hot. And electricity cost money. So everyone would have to take Freezing cold showers.

Cousin Squeakette and the rest of my relatives looked glum. No one noticed my sister, Thea, slip out of the room.

A minute later, she called up from the basement. "Uncle Samuel, great news!" she squeaked. "The hot-water heater isn't broken. The electricity was just SWITCHED OFF. Yep, it looks like there will be enough boiling hot water for everyone!"

Uncle Samuel S. Stingysnout's fur turned white. He slumped into a chair.

"Hot w-w-w-water, for everyone?" he gasped. "Someone bring me my smelling salts. I THINK I'M GOING TO FAINT!"

FRESHLY COOKED MUSSEL SOUP

After breakfast, Uncle Samuel invited everyone to play a round of golf, then archery, then Ping-Pong, then Tiddlywinks. It was clear he was trying to get our minds off food. Lunchtime came and went.

By three in the afternoon, we were all famished.

Trap stole into the kitchen and came back with a huge slice of cheese. It looked perfect. Perfectly delicious, that is. But when he bit into it, he chipped a tooth.

IT WAS MADE OF MARBLE!

That **night**, we all met around the dinner table.

"If that dude hasn't made some serious cheesy chow, my tail is, like, so outta here," my teenage cousin Skip Skatefur complained.

"I'm with you," Trap agreed. *"And I'm taking my wedding gifts with me!"*

Even my sweet Aunt Sugarfur nodded.

Everyone was fed up with being underfed!

At that moment, Uncle Samuel appeared at the door. He must have heard the comments because he looked slightly annoyed.

"Dear relatives, you must have noticed by now that I'm not exactly ROLLING in the dough," he squeaked. "The castle is in need of repairs. The garden is overgrown. And I had to fire the butler, the cook, the butcher, the baker, and the candlestick maker. But as Great-Grandfather Cheddar Cheapskate used to say, 'Don't judge a castle by its paint job.'"

The guests hung their heads. I guess everyone was feeling a little bit ashamed.

"Anyway," Uncle Samuel S. Stingysnout continued. "Since everyone is so hungry, I have decided to move the wedding ceremony up to **six** A.M. the day after tomorrow. You can all go home after that and stuff your snouts. There will be no reception or refreshments after the ceremony. After all, who can eat so early in the day?" he added with a chuckle. No one said a word.

The guests were either in shock or too weak to squeak.

Then Trap broke the silence. "Uncle Samuel," he said. "I get that you're low on the **CASH**,

but you must have scrounged something up for dinner tonight, right?"

Old Stingysnout beamed. "Ah, yes, my dear nephew, tonight I've gone all out." He waved a paw at Patience, who began passing out bowls of something or other.

What was inside? A parmesan shaving? A raisin?

But no, this time, Uncle Samuel S. Stingysnout really had outdone himself.

We were each presented with bowls of *steaming mussel soup.*

We gulped it down in no time flat.

Finally, a meal fit for a mouse.

CLANG! CLANG! CLANG!

That night, I woke up with a start. My tummy was rumbling away. IT MUST HAVE BEEN THE MUSSELS. I decided to go to the kitchen for a nice cup of warm milk.

I put on my clothes and wrapped a blanket around me.

Brrr. The castle felt just like a freezer.

I headed down the stairs. But just then, I heard a noise. Clang, clang, clang!

I stopped.

A light was shining in the castle's highest tower.

Clang, clang, clang!

I shivered. I shook. I twisted my tail up in knots.

Was it a ghost with chains? Was it a crazed cymbal-clanging monster?

I was scared. But I was curious.

I **climbed up** the stairs leading to the tower on shaky paws. Then I peeked through the keyhole.

Holey cheese! I couldn't believe it!

Uncle Samuel was sitting in a chair surrounded by a huge mound of gold coins. He was counting the coins one by one. Then he put them in stacks and dropped them into leather bags.

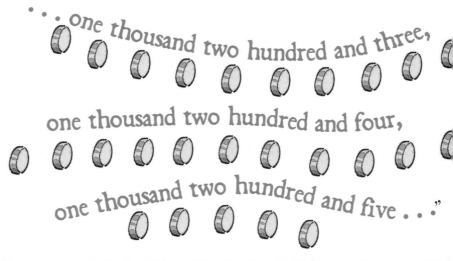

"...one thousand two hundred and three, one thousand two hundred and four, one thousand two hundred and five..."

Uncle Samuel was
counting the coins
one by one.

he counted, eyes shining with greed.

MOLDY MOZZARELLA! Where did all of this gold come from? Uncle Stingysnout's big speech about not rolling in the dough was all a LIE. And here I'd been feeling sorry for the old mouse! I guess he really did live up to his name.

I stood, frozen, unable to move. I couldn't tear my eyes away from Uncle Stingysnout. But right then, a door behind him opened.

WHAT'S WRONG WITH THE OLD ONES?

Stevie strolled into the room.

"Ah, look at all of this beautiful *gold*, my son," Uncle Samuel S. Stingysnout said, grinning. "Someday, this will all be yours. But you must promise me never to spend it on silly things like toilet paper or new underwear. What's wrong with the old ones, I say?"

Stevie put his paw on his **HEART**. "Of course, Father. I've been wearing the same underwear for five years. And toilet paper is for sissies," he agreed.

Old Stingysnout beamed.

"Great-Grandfather Cheapskate would be so proud, Son," he squeaked happily. "By the way, we'll have to **BUCKLE DOWN** and really save once these silly relatives have left. We've been spending too much on meals and water bills since they've been here."

I shook my head. I was in shock. Uncle Samuel had more money then Ratly Trump. Do you know him? He's the **wealthiest** business mouse on all of Mouse Island!

Quietly, I crept back to my room. The others were all awake. It seemed like everyone had an upset stomach.

"Do you know where the mussels came from?" moaned Trap. "**From the castle moat!** I overheard Old Stingysnout whispering to Stevie about them after dinner."

My fur stood on end. I wondered if a mouse could die from eating **poisoned shellfish**.

Thea decided that a little air would do us all good, so we climbed the stairs leading to the rooftop.

CHEAP WITH A CAPITAL "C"

Up on the roof, we heard someone crying. A small gray figure sat hunched over in the shadows.

It was Patience.

We walked over to her.

"What's wrong, bride-to-be?" Trap asked, trying to cheer her up. "You shouldn't be crying. You should be dancing. You're getting hitched to cousin Stevie the day after tomorrow!"

At the mention of the name Stevie, Patience began to cry harder.

"Oh, I'm so ashamed," she sobbed. "Stevie told me that I spend too much. He said I

need to learn how to save."

Thea rolled her eyes. She looked hotter with rage than a spicy cheese omelette at the Mexican Mouse Cantina. "Listen, Patience. I don't want to mess up your wedding plans, but you need to DROP that mouse like a sour cheese stick! He's mean. He's snotty. And he's cheap with a capital "C." You can find a million mice better than him!" she advised.

Patience blew her nose into a checkered handerchief. She looked miserable.

"But that's just it, Thea," she moaned. "I can't find another mouse. I'm not charming, or pretty, or witty like you. I'm just a plain old boring mouse. After my parents died, I felt all alone. I had no family. Then Stevie Stingysnout came along. I know he's just marrying me in hopes that he will find my family's money someday. But I guess he's better than no one."

"You know, Patience," Trap scoffed, "family really isn't all it's cracked up to be. I mean, take Geronimo, for example. Do you know how embarrassing it is to have a cousin like him?"

I tried to ignore him. But I'd had it with all of Trap's insults. *I'd had it with his pranks.* Soon we were chasing each other around the castle.

Patience watched us with teary eyes. "Ah, family. Even when you're fighting, you can tell how much you care about one another," I heard her tell Thea.

I glared at Trap. All I cared about was TWISTING his tail up in the biggest knot ever.

EXTREME MOUSE MAKEOVER

Thea put her paw around Patience. She led her inside. Then she ordered the rest of us to follow. I didn't argue. My sister can get pretty crabby when she doesn't get her way.

Thea had Patience stand in front of a full-length MIRROR. "Hmm, let's see," she said, examining Patience from head to pawnail. "What do you say we do a little makeover on you? It will make you feel like a million bucks."

Patience stared at her glum reflection. "I don't know, Thea," she said, sighing. "What can you do? I'm just a drab, boring mouse, and I'm afraid there's no changing that."

If any mouse knew anything about

*Patience stared at her
glum reflection.*

makeovers, it was my sister. She'd seen every episode of *Mouse Makeover* on the cable channel. It was her favorite show.

Now she took off Patience's eyeglasses. "First, we need to get you a pair of contacts. You have the most beautiful 𝖊𝖒𝖊𝖗𝖆𝖑𝖉 𝖌𝖗𝖊𝖊𝖓 eyes I've ever seen!" she squeaked. "And look at those long, shapely paws. You've been hiding them inside those awful granny dresses. I say, buy yourself some awesome miniskirts. Are you with me?"

Patience looked skeptical.

My sister didn't wait for an answer. She flung open Patience's closet and began ripping clothes off their hangers.

"𝖦𝖗𝖆𝖞, 𝖌𝖗𝖆𝖞, 𝖆𝖓𝖉 𝖒𝖔𝖗𝖊 𝖌𝖗𝖆𝖞! Oh, what a terrible color! From now on, you must not wear one more stitch of gray!" she instructed Patience. "You must wear green to bring out your eyes, or red to warm up your fur."

Patience nodded, overwhelmed. "Oh, of course, yes, whatever you say," she mumbled.

I smiled. No one can ever say no to my sister.

Thea gathered Patience's clothes together and chucked them all out the window.

"Now we're ready to get started!" she squeaked, putting a paw around Patience. "It's time for Thea Stilton's extra-fabumouse, extra-spectacular makeover. *When I'm done with you, my dear rodent, you won't even recognize yourself!*"

She pushed the rest of us out the door, screaming, "leave us alone!"

Then she hung up a sign. DO NOT DISTURB! ARTIST AT WORK!

WHAT A SIGHT!

The next morning, Patience and Thea headed for town. I watched them zoom off on Thea's motorcycle. What a sight! At first, Patience looked thrilled. Then she looked terrified. Of course, the three wheelies Thea did in the driveway probably didn't help calm her down.

Later that night, the pair returned. They were loaded down with lots of bags and PACKAGES of all shapes and sizes. We tried to sneak a peek at Patience, but she was too fast. The two rodents disappeared into the bride-to-be's room, giggling like school mice.

They even slammed the door on Stevie's snout. He stood in the hallway, looking stunned.

BEYOND GLAMOROUS

An hour later, I heard Thea's door open. A mouse shyly peeked out.

It wasn't Thea.

But it wasn't Patience Plainpaws either.

This mouse wasn't drab. *She was beyond glamorous!*

She had rich HONEY BLONDE FUR that fell in waves around her pretty face. She was dressed in a short silky red dress that showed off her long shapely paws. Her **GREEN EYES** sparkled under long lashes.

I blinked. Who was this **stunning beauty**? I took off my eyeglasses to clean them. Was I seeing things? Was this really Patience Plainpaws?

The small mouse took a few hesitant steps down the hallway.

"Ahem, how do I look, Geronimo?" she asked.

I gasped. It *was* Patience! I was about to tell her she was a vision of true beauty when Trap showed up.

"Somebody catch me! I think I'm about to faint!" he shrieked dramatically. "Who is this *babelicious* mouselette? Thea, why haven't you introduced us?"

My sister giggled. "Don't you recognize her, Cousin?" she squeaked. "IT'S PATIENCE, MY MAKEOVER MASTERPIECE!"

Trap took off like a shot. Then he returned with a red rose clamped between his teeth.

He threw himself on the floor in front of Patience. "What do you say, gorgeous? You and me, on a cruise to the Nibblette Islands? I know a great travel agent," he suggested.

I rolled my eyes. Trap was such a shameless *flirt*.

With a red rose clamped between his teeth, Trap threw himself on the floor in front of Patience.

"Ahem, dear Patience," I said, clearing my throat. "I have two tickets to the cheese rind exhibit at the New Mouse City Mouseum next week. I would love to take you."

Patience blushed. I guess she wasn't used to being noticed. She started to stammer something, but my sister cut her off.

"Listen, you two, my mouse here is very busy. I'm proud to say that her calendar is filled for the next three weeks!" she exclaimed.

I'M RICH!

Soon, we all followed Patience down to the living room. Suddenly, Stevie popped out from behind a column. When he saw Patience, his jaw hit the ground.

"Patience . . . what did you . . . how could you . . . how much **did this cost**?" he finally mumbled.

A look of disgust covered Patience's face. She put her paws on her hips.

She looked like a new mouse, confident and strong.

"That is so like you, Stevie," she said. "All you care about is money! Well, you won't have to worry about me anymore, because I'm breaking our engagement. I don't want to be married to a stingy old snot. I've realized that I deserve better, thanks to my new friend, Thea Stilton."

STEVIE GLARED AT THEA.

"Yes, Stevie dear, Patience needs more than a single bread crumb for breakfast," my sister explained. "She needs cheese danish once in a while and even a fancy dinner on the town now and then. She deserves kindness! She's sick of being cooped up here in this **dingy** old castle. She wants to meet new people and travel to exotic lands."

Now Stevie glared at Patience. **"EXOTIC LANDS?** And how do you think you're going to pay for that?" he smirked.

His *ex*-fiancée smiled shrewdly. "Oh, I forgot to tell you. Thea and I stopped at my parents' old mouse hole on our way to town. And guess what? I found their hidden fortune. I'm **RICH**!" She grinned.

At the thought of Patience's newfound money, Stevie's fur turned white. His eyes rolled back into his head. Then he fainted.

dinner on the town . . . meet new people . . . Cheese danish . . . travel to exotic lands . . . a fancy

BACK TO THE BIG CITY

Now that the wedding was off, everyone was free to leave. Guests shoved their belongings into suitcases and hightailed it out of there. I guess everyone had had enough of Old Stingysnout's castle. I, for one, couldn't wait to get home to my cozy mouse hole. As soon as I got there, I was going to make myself the biggest bowl of macaroni and cheese ever. *Delicious!*

We said good-bye to Patience on the castle steps. She was on her way out, too.

"Are you sure you don't want to come with me?" Trap asked the newly single mouse. "I'll take you to all of New Mouse City's **HOPPING** clubs. We can scamper the night away."

I pushed my cousin aside.

"Patience isn't interested in ratty nightclubs," I told Trap. Then I whispered in Patience's ear. "If you'd like, I can take you to my EXCLUSIVE golf club or to the opera," I offered.

Thea put her paw on Patience's arm. "Forget those two," she snickered. "I'll

Forget those two. I'll introduce you to my friends.

introduce you to my friends. They're smart, fun, and very adventurous. We'll have the most fabumouse time!"

Patience thought about it for a second. Then she grinned and jumped on the back of Thea's motorcycle.

The bike TOOK OFF with a deafening roar. As for the rest of us, let's just say we were left in the dust.

AN INTERESTING BUNCH

Several days later, I sat in my comfy pawchair at home thinking about the wedding. Well, actually, I wasn't really thinking about the wedding. After all, the wedding part never did happen. I was thinking about all of my crazy relatives. I flipped through T H E P H O T O S I had taken. Their faces grinned back at me.

There was Patience, before Thea's makeover. And Stevie, before Patience dumped him. There was Uncle Samuel looking as cheap as ever, and my dear Aunt Sugarfur, Uncle Kindpaws, Uncle Gagrat, and the rest of them.

I must say, we did make an interesting bunch.

But then, I guess all families are interesting in their own way . . . right?

Want to read my next adventure?
It's sure to be a fur-raising experience!

DOWN AND OUT
DOWN UNDER

G'day, mate! I was off on a fabumouse adventure — to Australia! But between surfing with sharks, being chased by poisonous snakes, and getting lost in the outback, I was beginning to wonder if this trip Down Under was really a good idea. Kangaroos and koalas and crocs — oh, my! Would I ever see New Mouse City again?

ABOUT THE AUTHOR

Born in New Mouse City, Mouse Island, Geronimo Stilton is Rattus Emeritus of Mousomorphic Literature and of Neo-Ratonic Comparative Philosophy. For the past twenty years, he has been running *The Rodent's Gazette*, New Mouse City's most widely read daily newspaper.

Stilton was awarded the Ratitzer Prize for his scoops on *The Curse of the Cheese Pyramid* and *The Search for Sunken Treasure*. He has also received the Andersen 2000 Prize for Personality of the Year. One of his bestsellers won the 2002 eBook Award for world's best ratlings' electronic book. His works have been published all over the globe.

In his spare time, Mr. Stilton collects antique cheese rinds and plays golf. But what he most enjoys is telling stories to his nephew Benjamin.

THE RODENT'S GAZETTE

1. Main entrance
2. Printing presses (where the books and newspaper are printed)
3. Accounts department
4. Editorial room (where the editors, illustrators, and designers work)
5. Geronimo Stilton's office
6. Storage space for Geronimo's books

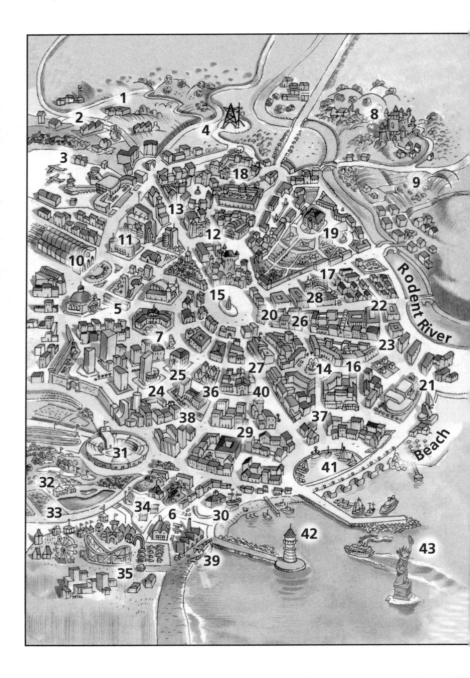

Map of New Mouse City

1. Industrial Zone
2. Cheese Factories
3. Angorat International Airport
4. WRAT Radio and Television Station
5. Cheese Market
6. Fish Market
7. Town Hall
8. Snotnose Castle
9. The Seven Hills of Mouse Island
10. Mouse Central Station
11. Trade Center
12. Movie Theater
13. Gym
14. Catnegie Hall
15. Singing Stone Plaza
16. The Gouda Theater
17. Grand Hotel
18. Mouse General Hospital
19. Botanical Gardens
20. Cheap Junk for Less (Trap's store)
21. Parking Lot
22. Mouseum of Modern Art
23. University and Library
24. *The Daily Rat*
25. *The Rodent's Gazette*
26. Trap's House
27. Fashion District
28. The Mouse House Restaurant
29. Environmental Protection Center
30. Harbor Office
31. Mousidon Square Garden
32. Golf Course
33. Swimming Pool
34. Blushing Meadow Tennis Courts
35. Curlyfur Island Amusement Park
36. Geronimo's House
37. New Mouse City Historic District
38. Public Library
39. Shipyard
40. Thea's House
41. New Mouse Harbor
42. Luna Lighthouse
43. The Statue of Liberty

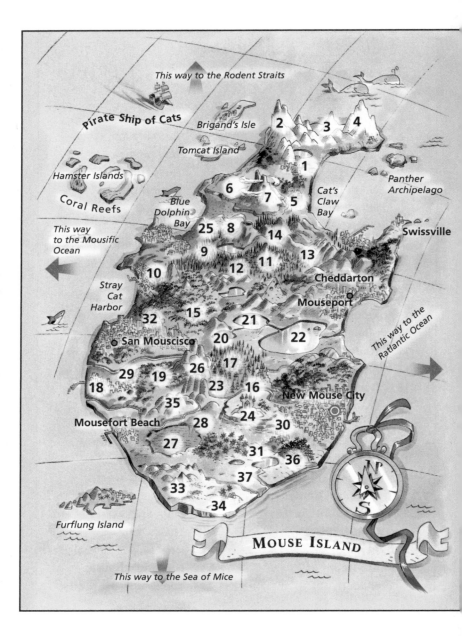

This way to the Rodent Straits

Pirate Ship of Cats

Brigand's Isle

Tomcat Island

2

3

4

1

Hamster Islands

Coral Reefs

Blue
Dolphin
Bay

6

7

5

Cat's
Claw
Bay

Panther
Archipelago

This way
to the Mousific
Ocean

25

8

14

Swissville

9

13

10

12

11

Cheddarton

Stray
Cat
Harbor

15

Mouseport

32

21

22

This way to the
Ratlantic Ocean

San Mouscisco

20

17

29

26

19

23

16

New Mouse City

18

35

24

30

28

Mousefort Beach

27

31

36

33

37

34

Furflung Island

MOUSE ISLAND

N

E

W

S

This way to the Sea of Mice

Map of Mouse Island

1. Big Ice Lake
2. Frozen Fur Peak
3. Slipperyslopes Glacier
4. Coldcreeps Peak
5. Ratzikistan
6. Transratania
7. Mount Vamp
8. Roastedrat Volcano
9. Brimstone Lake
10. Poopedcat Pass
11. Stinko Peak
12. Dark Forest
13. Vain Vampires Valley
14. Goose Bumps Gorge
15. The Shadow Line Pass
16. Penny Pincher Castle
17. Nature Reserve Park
18. Las Ratayas Marinas
19. Fossil Forest
20. Lake Lake
21. Lake Lakelake
22. Lake Lakelakelake
23. Cheddar Crag
24. Cannycat Castle
25. Valley of the Giant Sequoia
26. Cheddar Springs
27. Sulfurous Swamp
28. Old Reliable Geyser
29. Vole Vale
30. Ravingrat Ravine
31. Gnat Marshes
32. Munster Highlands
33. Mousehara Desert
34. Oasis of the Sweaty Camel
35. Cabbagehead Hill
36. Rattytrap Jungle
37. Rio Mosquito

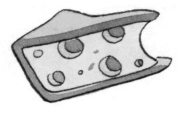

Don't miss any of my other fabumouse adventures!

#1 Lost Treasure of the Emerald Eye

#2 The Curse of the Cheese Pyramid

#3 Cat and Mouse in a Haunted House

#4 I'm Too Fond of My Fur!

#5 Four Mice Deep in the Jungle

#6 Paws Off, Cheddarface!

#7 Red Pizzas for a Blue Count

#8 Attack of the Bandit Cats

#9 A Fabumouse Vacation for Geronimo

#10 All Because of a Cup of Coffee

#11 It's Halloween, You 'Fraidy Mouse!

#12 Merry Christmas, Geronimo!

#13 The Phantom of the Subway

#14 The Temple of the Ruby of Fire

#15 The Mona Mousa Code

#16 A Cheese-Colored Camper

#17 Watch Your Whiskers, Stilton!

#18 Shipwreck on the Pirate Islands

#19 My Name Is Stilton, Geronimo Stilton

#20 Surf's Up, Geronimo!

#21 The Wild, Wild West

#22 The Secret of Cacklefur Castle

A Christmas Tale

#23 Valentine's Day Disaster

#24 Field Trip to Niagara Falls

#25 The Search for Sunken Treasure

#26 The Mummy with No Name

#27 The Christmas Toy Factory

and coming soon

#29 Down and Out Down Under

Dear mouse friends,
Thanks for reading, and farewell
till the next book.
It'll be another whisker-licking-good
adventure, and that's a promise!

Geronimo Stilton